The Christmas Coat

by CLYDE ROBERT BULLA

illustrated by

SYLVIE WICKSTROM

ALFRED A. KNOPF   NEW YORK

THIS IS A BORZOI BOOK PUBLISHED BY ALFRED A. KNOPF, INC.

Text copyright © 1989 by Clyde Robert Bulla.
Illustrations copyright © 1989 by Sylvie Wickstrom.

Manufactured in the United States of America
Book design by Mina Greenstein
2   4   6   8   10   9   7   5   3   1

Library of Congress Cataloging-in-Publication Data
Bulla, Clyde Robert. The Christmas coat / by Clyde Robert Bulla ; pictures by
Sylvie Wickstrom.   p.   cm.
Summary: Two brothers who squabble all the time cause their mother great despair, until a
common purpose unites them in working unselfishly together—enabling them to give their
mother her dearest wish for Christmas.
ISBN 0-394-89385-9   ISBN 0-394-99385-3 (lib. bdg.)
[1. Brothers—Fiction.   2. Christmas—Fiction]   I. Wickstrom, Sylvie, ill.   II. Title.
PZ7.B912Cj   1990   [E]—dc19   88-2380

THERE WERE three in the family. Once there had been four, but Papa had gone away. He had gone to war and never come back. Mama and the two boys were left.

To earn their bread, Mama worked in other people's houses. Every evening she came home to care for the boys, Hans and Otto. Every morning she sent them off to school.

People in the village called her a brave woman.

She did not feel brave. Many times she wanted to sit down and cry.

She had tried hard to make a good home, but they were not a happy family. There was no peace between the boys. Day after day they quarreled. Sometimes they fought.

"Can't you be good?" she would say. "For just one day, can't you be *good*?"

"Mama, I *am* good," Otto would say. "It is Hans who makes the trouble."

"Mama, Otto will not listen to me," Hans would say. "I am a year older, and he should listen."

One evening she came home to find them fighting. They were on the floor. A chair was tipped over. A dish was broken.

"Enough!" she cried.

They got up.

"Otto tried to push me down," said Hans.

"No, he tried to push *me*," said Otto.

"I have heard all this before. I'll have no more of it."

Mama sent Hans to one side of the room. She sent Otto
to the other. Then, with a piece of chalk, she drew a line
across the floor.

"There," she said. "Hans, you have your side of the
room. Otto, you have yours. When you come from school,
each of you will stay on his own side. You will stay till I
come home."

So, when Mama was away, each one kept to his side of
the room. But they could talk over the line.

Christmas was coming.

"I have Christmas money," said Hans.

"So have I," said Otto.

"I have more than you," said Hans.

They had shoveled snow for their teacher. He had paid them each five pennies.

Otto had bought a cake with one of his pennies.

"You had to have a sugar cake with jelly on top," said Hans. "Now you have only four pennies because you are a greedy pig."

Otto said nothing.

"I'm going to buy a Christmas gift for Mama," said Hans.

"So am I," said Otto.

"I'm going to buy her a comb," said Hans. "I saw it in the store window. It is gold with diamonds in it."

"I'm going to buy her a handkerchief with strawberries on it," said Otto.

"But my gift will be better," said Hans, "because I have five pennies and you have only four."

Otto was so angry he pulled off his shoe and threw it at his brother.

"Ha, you missed me," said Hans.

Mama came home. "How did that shoe get there?" she asked.

"He threw it at me," said Hans.

"He called me a name," said Otto.

"What can I do with such boys?" cried Mama. "What can I *do*?"

It was three days till Christmas.

Hans and Otto came home from school. There was a box on the table. It was a big box tied with green ribbon.

"It's from Mama," said Otto.

"She said there would be no gifts this year," said Hans. But there was the box.

They looked at it. Hans put out his hand.

"Don't you touch it," said Otto.

"I will if I want to. It's on my side of the room." Hans touched the box. He picked it up.

"Put it down," said Otto. "It's not yours."

"Maybe it is." Hans pulled at the ribbon.

"Don't you open it!" cried Otto.

The ribbon came untied.

Otto shouted. He stamped his feet. "You'd better not—!"

But Hans had the box open. He was looking inside.

"Well? Well?" From his side of the room, Otto tried to see. "What *is* it?"

"I won't tell you," said Hans.

Otto came over the line. He looked into the box. Inside was a coat.

It was made of soft red wool. There were shiny black buttons down the front.

Otto looked under it. He had thought there might be two, but there was only one. One beautiful, red wool coat.

"Mama got it for me," said Hans.

"She did not," said Otto.

"Yes, she did," said Hans, "because I help her more."

"You do *not* help her more!" shouted Otto.

"You're on my side of the room. Get back." Hans gave his brother a push. "I'm going to try on my coat."

He started to put it on.

Otto caught hold of it. They were both pulling at the coat. Suddenly it ripped up the back. They had almost torn it in two!

Hans said, "There! See what you did."

Otto said, "See what *you* did."

Hans put the coat back into the box. He tied the ribbon.

"Why are you doing that?" asked Otto.

"So Mama won't know," said Hans.

"She *will* know," said Otto.

They were not shouting now. They were talking very quietly.

Mama came home.

"I'm late," she said. "I stopped to see Hilda. Oh, it will be a happy Christmas at her house."

Hilda was their neighbor.

"I saw Karl, too," said Mama. "He was out of bed and *walking*."

Karl was Hilda's little boy. He had been ill for a long time. All his hair had come out. Now he was better. His hair was growing in again.

"Hilda brought the box over this morning," said Mama.

"The b-box?" said Hans.

"Yes, the box," she said. "Don't tell me you didn't see it. She wants us to keep it till Christmas. It's a surprise for Karl."

"For *Karl?*" said Otto.

Mama put the box away in the cupboard. "It's a coat," she told them. "Old Maxim the tailor made it. Hilda didn't say how much it cost, but it took her ever so long to save the money. We'll see it on Christmas Day. Hilda wants us to bring it over."

She said to them at supper, "You're not eating. Are you sick?"

"No, Mama," said Otto.

"Just not very hungry," said Hans.

IN THE morning they walked to school together.

"You had to be the smart one and open the box," said Otto.

"You had to come over the line and tear the coat," said Hans.

"*You* tore it," said Otto. "And you thought it was yours. Couldn't you see it wasn't big enough? Stupid!"

"Stupid, yourself," said Hans. "Couldn't *you* see?"

That evening they waited at home for Mama. Otto began again, "You had to open the box—"

"Oh, stop," said Hans. "I'm trying to think."

"You have a lot to think about," said Otto. "You've spoiled Christmas for everyone—Karl and Hilda and Mama and us."

"What do you want me to do?" said Hans. "Take the blame?"

"Yes!" said Otto.

"I'm older, and I did open the box," said Hans, "so I'll take *some* of the blame. There! Does that make you feel better?"

Otto stared at him. Never before had his brother taken the blame for anything.

"So what are we going to do?" asked Hans.

"What *can* we do?" said Otto.

Then Mama came home, and they were quiet.

As they walked to school in the morning Otto said, "If we had some pins, we could pin up the tear in the coat."

"No," said Hans. "We couldn't make it look right."

At noon the boys and girls sat by the stove to eat their lunches. Hans sat down by Otto. The others began to whisper, "Now the fight begins."

But there was no fight. The two brothers talked, with their heads together.

"Maxim the tailor made the coat," said Hans. "Maybe he could mend it for us."

"Do you think he would?" asked Otto.

"We can ask," said Hans.

He went to the teacher. "'If you please, sir," he said, "may Otto and I go home a little early?"

"Have you a note from your mother?" asked the teacher.

"No, sir," said Hans. "This is about something we didn't want her to know."

The teacher was smiling. "Something about Christmas? Something about a gift?"

"Yes, sir," answered Hans.

"Then you may go a little early," said the teacher, "but just this once."

Hans and Otto went home. Otto took the box down from the cupboard. Hans untied the ribbon. Otto took out the coat and put it into a sack. Hans tied up the box again and put it back into the cupboard.

They ran all the way to the tailor shop. Old Maxim was sewing some cloth. He looked tired, and his eyes were red.

"If you please—" began Hans.

"Yes, yes," said the tailor.

Hans held up the coat.

The old man turned pale.

"We didn't mean to do it," said Otto.

"We thought if you could mend it before Christmas," said Hans, "no one would know."

"So you thought that," said the tailor. "You take my work and rip and tear it. Now you bring it for me to mend—in time for Christmas, if you please. Does your mother know what you have done?"

"No, sir," said Hans.

"Then take it home and show her," said the tailor. "Let her punish you as you *should* be punished!"

"Please," said Otto, "we don't want her to know. She works in other people's houses, and she comes home tired, and we make life hard for her. I don't know why, but we do, and I—I am as bad as my brother!"

"If you could try to mend it," said Hans, "I can pay. See?"

He took out his money and put it down on the worktable.

"You think my work is worth only five pennies?" said the tailor.

"I have money too," said Otto. He took out his pennies and put them down beside his brother's.

The tailor opened his mouth and closed it. He took the coat and held it up. "I don't know," he said. "Leave it and come back tomorrow. I'll see what can be done."

The NEXT day was the day before Christmas. After school Hans and Otto ran through the snow to the tailor shop.

Maxim had the coat in the sack. "I have done the best I could," he said.

"Thank you, thank you," said Hans and Otto.

"I want no thanks," the tailor said in a cross voice. "Take it and go."

They ran home. They took the coat out of the sack.

"Look how he mended it," said Hans.

"You could never tell," said Otto.

They put the coat into the box. Hans tied the ribbon. All the time they listened for Mama.

When she came home, the box was out of sight in the cupboard.

Mama gave them supper. "Only bread and milk," she said, "but there will be more tomorrow. Tomorrow I don't go to work. We will have all Christmas Day together."

IN THE morning they went to Hilda's. Karl was still in bed. His mother put the box under the Christmas tree. Then they watched him get up and find it.

He opened the box. "It's a coat!" he cried. "Now I can go play in the snow. Look, everybody. See my new coat!"

Hilda gave them all Christmas cakes, and Mama and Hans and Otto went home.

"Karl was so happy," said Mama. "He never had a new coat before."

"Here is something for you," said Hans, and he held out his hand with nothing in it. "It's a gold comb with diamonds."

"And this is from me," said Otto. "It's make-believe too. It's a handkerchief with strawberries."

"Maybe next Christmas we'll have real gifts," said Hans.

"You've already given me a real gift," said Mama. "It's what I've always wanted. I wished you would be good for just one day, and you have been good for *two*."

"We haven't been good, Mama," said Hans.

"Not good at all," said Otto.

"Of course you have. You think I don't know? You have stopped your quarreling and fighting. I don't know what happened, but you are good boys now." She brought a brush from the kitchen. She went down on her knees.

"What are you doing?" asked Hans.

"Scrubbing the floor on Christmas Day!" said Otto.

Then they saw that she was scrubbing out the chalk line on the floor.

"We don't need this now, do we?" she said.

Hans and Otto looked at each other.

"No, Mama," said Hans.

"No, Mama," said Otto.

They began to help her. They scrubbed out the chalk line with their shoes. It looked as if they were doing a funny dance.

E   Bulla, Clyde Robert   3962
BUL
                     The Christmas coat

$13.95

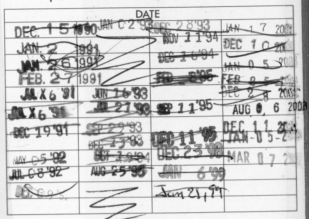

DATE			
DEC. 1 5 1990	JAN 0 2 '93	DEC 2 8 '93	JAN 1 7 200?
JAN. 2 1991		NOV 1 1 '94	DEC 1 0 20?
JAN 2 6 1991		DEC 1 6 '94	JAN 0 5 20?
FEB. 2 7 1991		FEB 8 '95	FEB 2 5 ?
JUL X 6 '91	JUN 1 6 '93		DEC 2 8 200?
JUL X 6 '91	JUL 2 7 '93	SEP 1 1 '95	AUG 0 6 200?
DEC 1 9 '91	SEP 2 9 '93		DEC 1 1 20?
	DEC 1 7 '93	DEC 1 1 '95	JAN 0 5 2?
MAY 0 5 '92	NOV 1 9 '94	DEC 2 3 '98	MAR 0 7 2?
JUL 0 8 '92	AUG 2 5 '95	JAN 6 '99	
DEC 2 9 '?		Jan 21, 94	